THE GOLDEN

THE GOLDEN
By
I Gilmour

Copyright © Ian Gilmour 2011

All of the characters and events in this book are fictitious, and any resemblance to actual persons, living or dead, is purely coincidental.

This book is an adventure story full of sex, violence and adult humour.

All rights reserved. No part of this publication may be reproduced, stored in a retrieval system, or transmitted in any form or by any means, electronic, mechanical, photo copying, recording, or otherwise, without the prior permission of the publisher.

Copies of this book are available from Amazon Kindle e-book Library.

1st edition published November 2011

2nd edition published February 2013

Author Ian Gilmour
Ig2002@hotmail.co.uk

THE GOLDEN GOBBLER 1
By
Ian Gilmour

Introduction

This is the story about an explorer and soldier of fortune called Casey Jones and his perilous quest to find the Golden Gobbler.
The Golden Gobbler is a statue of the first High Priestess of the Twatolo tribe. The figure is made of gold and diamonds and is priceless.

Legend has it the statue also has strange and magical powers.
However no explorers seeking the Golden Gobbler have ever been heard of again.
The statue is believed to be inside a secret temple somewhere in the forbidden territories on the other side of Deep Throat Valley.

No one knows how the statue came to be named the Golden Gobbler. One theory is that it was named after the first High Priestess of the Twatolo tribe, who was called Munchalot.
Another theory is that when the tribe were performing their ritual dances, they looked and sounded like wild turkeys.
However the true reason remains a mystery.

THE GOLDEN GOBBLER 1
By Ian Gilmour

CHAPTER 1
THE QUEST

Casey Jones is in his tree hut preparing to go on a perilous expedition deep into the forbidden territories.

This is place of great danger where no previous explorers have ever returned from or been heard of again.

His quest is to find the Golden Gobbler.

He hears the now familiar whistling noise and dives to the floor of the hut, but not quickly enough. An arrow with a message attached slices through his ear and takes off half of it.

"The jungle mail has arrived."

He looks at his severed ear and cries out in pain.

"Bollocks, I will be nicknamed eighteen months."(an ear and a half).

He reaches out for his bloody ear in the hope of sewing it back on again, but a passing monkey swings low, grabs the ear and eats it.

Casey is enraged and tries to shoot the thieving monkey, but the animal has disappeared into the trees. He stems the flow of blood and looks at the arrow embedded in the wall of the tree hut. He reads the attached note.

THE GOLDEN GOBBLER 1

It is a message from the Umbollock tribe, who are the only tribe native to the area that he has befriended. They have agreed to supply him with two of their best warriors to act as guides for part of the way. However they will only take him as far as the entrance to Deep Throat Valley, as they are too scared to go any further. They will meet him at their village tomorrow at dawn.

Casey meets them as planned and they set off on their perilous expedition. He relates what happens on the way.

The first day of the expedition is hazardous and takes the life of one of the guides. When we were making our way along the trail, the guide unfortunately sets off a booby trap laid in our path, and a wooden stake shoots through his neck killing him instantly.

Witnessing this, the other guide keeps slowing up encouraging me to go first. I get pissed off with this, and shoot him dead. I must make the dangerous journey on my own now.

Then I have a brilliant idea. I take out my trusty jungle knife, the blade of which is made from an ancient warrior's knee replacement and honed to razor sharpness. I cut off the guides head and tie a rope around it, then coil the rope around the head and use it like a yo-yo, reeling it back and forward in my path to set off any more hidden booby traps.

This works superbly, I make good time and soon arrive at the entrance to Deep Throat Valley.

I am tired and decide to camp here for the night. I get a fire going and have a meal of fried monkey brains with a packet of crisps and a tomato to follow. I sense something or someone watching.

THE GOLDEN GOBBLER 1

Quick as a flash I dive for cover as an arrow flies over my head. I grab my machine-gun and fire a few rounds in the direction the arrow came from. More arrows fly in from all directions. I recognise the arrows, they are from the Umbollock tribe. They must have discovered their dead guides and are not too happy with me. I move to better cover, firing my machine-gun and hitting a few by the sound of their screams.

I am surrounded, more arrows fly in and it looks like the end. "But not yet." I have an ace card up my sleeve that had worked before. I grab my tape recorder that has a recording of my sister singing "I belong to Glasgow" while she was pissed up on wine and vodka. I play the recording at full volume and hear the tormented screams of the Umbollocks as they run away in fear and terror. "Good old sis, you saved my bacon for sure this time." The way now seems clear for me to continue with my quest.

I make ready to set off on the trail again. Before I go, I have a piss against a tree. I see a dark shadow rising up from the base of the tree, accompanied by hissing and rattling. I turn my head to see an enormous snake with blood red eyes and yellow venom dripping from its fangs. It has its head back ready to strike. This is a life or death situation. I must act with haste.

Quick as a flash I point my own trouser snake (which has a tattoo of a skull and crossbones on the end) at the hissing reptile. On seeing this, the snake recoils in horror and fear and slithers away at great speed into the jungle undergrowth. I give my friend a thankful shake and journey onwards.

THE GOLDEN GOBBLER 1

I make my way along Deep Throat Valley reeling out old yo-yo head in front in case there are any more hidden booby traps, when suddenly the ground in front moves. A root like object bursts through the earth, multiplying all around. They are bright red, twisting and curling, snaking their way along the ground towards me.

No escape, one wraps securely around my ankle, tightening and crushing. A horrendous pain ensues as I try to break free. I manage to reach my razor sharp machete, the blade of which is made from an ancient warriors hip replacement, and the bone handle fashioned from my grandmothers old corset.

I quickly cut through the root like tendril. Yellow acid like liquid spews from the severed end, burning and destroying anything it comes into contact with. Another root wraps around my neck, crushing and choking me. I slice through this also, and an agonising pain follows as the yellow spewing acid hits my neck. Between the trees I see a glowing red large circular object. "Is this controlling the things trying to kill me?" I quickly fire a round from my grenade launcher and score a direct hit. A massive fireball ensues as the sphere shaped object explodes and the root like tendrils lies dormant and dead.

I take stock of the situation. "Bruises and burns on various parts of my body, thinking to myself "That was a close shave," good old lady luck was on my side this time." I continue along the trail reeling out old yo-yo head as I go. There is an eerie silence in this place, I sense something is near. I take evasive action and get off the trail into the dense undergrowth of the jungle.

THE GOLDEN GOBBLER 1

I climb a tree and wait. After a few minutes, I hear sounds from below. I look down and see a creature moving slowly towards the tree I have climbed up. The beast has reached the base of the tree and looks upwards. It knows I am there. The creature is the size of a large grizzly bear, but its head is like a sabre tooth tiger's. With a great roar, the beast starts climbing the tree. Huge claws are stripping the bark of the tree as it gets closer.

Quick as a flash, I fire forty rounds from my machine-gun into the body of the attacking animal. Still it races towards me. It grabs hold of my leg. I drive my trusty jungle knife into one of the creature's eyes. This does the trick, and the beast falls to earth. I climb down from the tree.

The beast is dead. I can once more continue with my quest to find the Golden Gobbler."

I find the trail again, and proceed along very cautiously, rolling out old yo-yo head as I go. I have travelled for miles and now I have no water left. I see drops of water fall from the valley wall. The drops turn into a trickle. I then quickly stick my head under and take in a mouthful. It is warm and tastes foul. I spit out the putrid liquid. I look up through the vegetation and see a painted warrior standing on a ledge above. He is unaware I am below. He is pissing over the edge. I curse, "Bollocks." I spit again. This is where the water is coming from.

I recognise the pissers war paint; he is a twat of the Twatolo tribe. This is the oldest tribe native to these parts and they are not a very friendly bunch of fellows. I have to find out if there are any more of them around the valley.

THE GOLDEN GOBBLER 1

I make my way back along the trail and climb up onto the ridge above. I sneak up on the pissing twat and when I am about twenty feet away I unleash old yo yo head, striking the warriors head and knocking him out cold. I quickly bind his hands and feet. When he regains consciousness I question him in his native tongue.

"How many Twatolum in um valley-um?"

"We no take um drugs" was his smart arsed reply.
I give him a sharp tap on the nose with old yo-yo head splitting and breaking skin and bone. I ask him again,

"How many Twatolum in um valley-um?"

"Fuck-um off-um," was the brave warriors reply.
I smile as I remember the old saying.

"Fortune Favours the Brave."
Unfortunately for him, he met me today. Fortune was not on his side as I quickly slit his throat. I take his water supply and one of his ears to replace the one I lost.

I make my way along the ridge and see smoke to my left. I approach with caution. In the middle of the trees is a Twatolo village of wood and straw huts. Around the fire are about fifty painted warriors. In a corner is a captured golden skinned beauty of oriental appearance tied to a post. I have to rescue her and save her from a terrible fate. It is getting dark. The Twatolo warriors put their captive into a hut with her hands and feet tied. A warrior is standing guard at the front of the hut. I sneak round to the back and silently cut an entry hole and go inside.

THE GOLDEN GOBBLER 1

"Have you come to rescue me?" asks the girl. "Yes, but you must be very quiet," I reply. I cut her loose from her bonds.

"I am velly glateful" she says, and smiles as she opens her legs.

I have to think fast as we must get away from here as soon as possible, but then again, I have been in the jungle alone for six months. Then I have a brilliant idea.

Quick as a flash I plug in old Jolly Roger and tell the girl to wrap her legs tightly round my waist and her arms around my neck. I hot foot it out of the village and have the added advantage that the oriental beauty can look over my shoulder to see if anyone follows. When we get well clear of the village, she finishes showing her gratitude against a tree.

We must make haste, the Twatolo warriors are sure to be hopping mad when they discover she is missing. Also they won't be over fond of me when they find one of their twats with his throat cut. I decide to give old yo-yo head a rest, and tell my rescued companion to run along the trail in front of me in case there are any more hidden booby traps. She is not happy with this and complains bitterly.

"Me no wanna go first, it too dangerous."

"Don't be so ungrateful," I reply, and prod her along with Jolly Roger who is still at half-mast.

After about two hours travel, we stop and I check my map. I need to find the twin peaked mountain. That is where I will find the entrance to the temple that holds the Golden Gobbler and all her mysterious secrets.

9

THE GOLDEN GOBBLER 1

I scan the area with my binoculars. I spot the twin peaked mountain in the distance.

I say aloud, "The Golden Gobbler is near."

"Me here," says my golden skinned companion on her knees in front of me tugging at my zip.

"Ah well, while you're down there." I laugh.

"And by the way, what's yer name?"

"Turkey Head." she replies.

"That figures." I say to her.

She takes out Jolly Roger and jumps back in fright when she sees the tattoo of the skull and crossbones on the end.

"It no bite me?" she asks.

I assure her, "No, if you no bite, Jolly Roger no bite." While she is showing her gratitude I make myself a drink. I pour some whiskey into a glass and then some water. I hold this on top of the oriental beauty's bobbing head to mix it up. I drink it down in one gulp. My companion also has a drink and we make ready to set off on the journey once again.

"Right let's get going Turkey Head, you lead the way, up the front of the trail you go." She is not happy with this and complains again. "Me no wanna go in front, me nearly fell over the cliff last time." Being a compassionate type of person I tell her I will make it easier for her. I tie old yo-yo head loosely round her neck and stand behind her holding the rope end. "If you fall over the cliff I will pull you back up." "Happy now?"

"Me no like smelly head." she replies.

"You never complained earlier." I remind her.

I was starting to get annoyed with Miss Turkey head and reach for my trusty jungle knife.

THE GOLDEN GOBBLER 1

On reflection, I remember I need a cook, so I decide to let her live. (For now.) No wonder there has been no sign of the Twatolo chasing us, maybe they were glad to be rid of her. I roll up old yo-yo head and point my gun at moaning Minnie. "Now move or die here." She gets the message and quickly runs along the trail in front. I hear the crack of the trees breaking in the wind followed by a scream from the trail ahead.

My companion has been caught in a booby trap. She is hanging upside down with a rope around one ankle and dangling about twenty feet in the air. This trap was meant to capture alive and not to kill.

I am in a deadly situation now. A warrior attacks from my left, I dive to the side as his hatchet narrowly misses my head as he swings it in my direction. My trusty jungle knife is soon in action once more. Quick as a flash I slash open his guts, then my razor sharp machete slices off his head with ease. I look at the head and cry out, "Bollocks!" This is not a twat of the Twatolo tribe; this is a hundred times worse.

I recognise the tattoo design across the warrior's forehead. It is that of a closed fist with a snakes head popping out above it. This warrior is a wanker of the Wankoora tribe.

The Wankoora are sadistic cannibals who torture their captives, keeping them alive for as long as possible while cutting off bits of body to eat. There is no way I want to be captured alive by this lot.

THE GOLDEN GOBBLER 1

I grab my machine gun as the attack begins in earnest. Now more Wankoora attack from all sides, the situation is looking rather bleak. I spray the area with bullets. There are loud explosions followed by screams and shouting. I guess some attackers have been killed and injured, blown up by the grenade and trip-wire booby traps that I had rigged up on the trail behind earlier.

Spears are coming at me from the trail in front. I see more attacking Wankoora and open fire with my machine gun; I throw a grenade in for good measure. Still they come at me through the trees. I shoot them down. Then I remember that the Wankoora cover their skin with animal fat to avoid being discovered while hunting. Quick as a flash I grab my trusty flame-thrower and spray an arc over the dry undergrowth. Intense flames spread quickly. The screams of the dying warriors can be heard along with the spitting fat as they burn and sizzle in their skins.

By now all around is ablaze, apart from the trail ahead. I check out the situation. There are dead wankers lying all around, or so it appears. I take no chances, I roll out old yo-yo head across the bodies. One wanker playing dead jumps up raising his spear, one bullet between the eyes and one in the mouth quieten him down. The other attackers are all dead. I go back and cut the rope to free Turkey Head who has been watching the fun from above. She is frightened and excited at the same time.

THE GOLDEN GOBBLER 1

"Me velly glateful you rescue me again," she says, as she opens her legs.

"No, not now, we must keep moving." I tell her.

"OK," she says, "me no argue, you very dangerous if anybody upsets you."

"What you called?" she asks

"You can call me Master, and I will call you Goldie, for Turkey Head is no name for a lady."

I pat and stroke her ass. "Where did this ass come from Goldie?" "Out of the trees," she replies. "That's good the beast can carry the supplies, also it can come back with us when we return. I will give it to my daughter as a gift, I will tell her it's a pony, she won't know the difference; it also grieves me to see you struggling along the trail carrying my rucksack and all the supplies."

"Can the ass not go in front?" asks Goldie.

"No, you go in front in case there are any more booby traps, I will keep the ass with me in case I get tired, then the beast can carry me along for a bit." I can still hear the now distant screams of the Wankoora as they burn and fry in the fiery forest.

Suddenly a hand holding a club shoots out of the ass's ass. This is not a real ass; it is a Trojan ass with wankers hidden inside. Before I can move I am clubbed unconscious. When I awake both myself and Goldie are tied to a post. We are prisoners of the Wankoora tribe. In front of me is a wanker standing guard. The others are asleep around a fire. In the centre is a large pot filled with boiling liquid.

THE GOLDEN GOBBLER 1

The guard is mad with anger and shakes his fist. "You very nasty man, you kill many Wankoora, and your trollop killed three with her Kung Fu. Now only ten wankers survive." You both go in cooking pot, then we eat you, but before that, we torture you plenty, slice off skin, and break many bones." He laughs aloud, "ha ha..h

He never finishes the third ha. I see his head bounce and roll along the ground towards me. His headless body falls to earth, blood spraying everywhere. Behind him is standing a frightening figure with spiked red hair, blue and white war paint cover her face, wild staring bloodshot eyes scan the area. She holds a razor sharp samurai sword with blood still dripping from the blade.

This can only be the feared Mad Mary from Macedonia and her band of marauding minstrels who fiddle as they kill. Her gang of evil rat like creatures have already captured the rest of the Wankoora warriors and have them bound and tied up in a line.

I thank Mad Mary as she cuts us free. She faintly resembles my own darling daughter. But it can't be, for she is thousands of miles away playing the Harp and making sweet gentle music.

The fiddler starts playing the wild music. Mad Mary from Macedonia grabs her thunder-box, and screeching like a crazy chimpanzee, she belts out the music of the Underworld. The rest of her band joins in. The killing will happen soon I think, as the music reaches fever point. However the Wankoora prisoners can stand the evil strains no longer and hop over to the bubbling boiling cauldron and throw themselves in, screaming with madness as they go.

THE GOLDEN GOBBLER 1

With that the music stops. Mad Mary and her band of marauding minstrels make ready to go. Before they depart she says.

"Be more careful in future Casey Jones, and ditch the trollop, she brings you bad luck." Then they were gone, disappearing silently into the dense jungle. I take into account what Mad Mary has said, but I decide to keep Goldie with me as a companion and to carry the supplies. I also decide I would like to give her one before we set off again. She must have read my mind, for as I look round she is lying on her back, naked with her legs apart. I quickly run over to her, dropping my trousers as I go. I get one leg out, but in my haste I unfortunately trip over, fall and hit my head on a rock.

When I regain consciousness, Goldie has very kindly tended to my cut head, and put a bandage round it. Due to me having a headache, I decide to leave sex till later. We gather some supplies and set off on the trail again. After travelling for about five minutes my companion stops on the trail ahead.

"What's wrong?" I ask her.

"Me wanna crap," she replies.

"Do it over the edge of the cliff."

I was also just about to tell her to hold onto something when I see her plummet arse first over the cliff down into the deep valley below.

THE GOLDEN GOBBLER 1

I run over to the cliff edge, but there is no sign of her, all I can hear are her far distant screams as she drops down into the abyss below.

I ponder for a moment to say a few words of tribute and fond farewell to my golden skinned beautiful companion.

"Tough luck Goldie, you shit out there big style."

I then continue with my quest to find the Golden Gobbler.

THE GOLDEN GOBBLER 1

CHAPTER 2

MONKS AND MERCENERIES

I make my way cautiously along the trail, reeling out old yo-yo head in front for my protection. So far so good, I am making good progress, and there have been no further booby traps in my way. I have now reached the end of the trail on the ridge. I check my position and scan the area to get my bearings.

I see the twin peaked mountain on the other side of the valley. "This is where I must go." I make my way down from the ridge to meet up with the trail below. I see movement from the right. I take cover and watch the approaching procession.

As they get near I recognise the group by their pink robes and shaven heads. They are Nobu monks from the Nobulot monastery, many miles from here.

The Nobu monks are a strange lot who combine prayer and physical exercise. They do this by one monk lying spread-eagled on the ground and the second monk doing press ups on his back.

This all seems a bit dodgy to me.

"What can they be doing so far from home I wonder?" However they are known to be a happy and friendly bunch of chaps, so I approach to meet them.

THE GOLDEN GOBBLER 1

I call out to them. "Greetings Nobu monks." They stop and the head Nobber falls to the ground and lies spread-eagled.

"No no! I don't want to join you in prayer and physical exercise, I am only saying hello."

"What are you doing here?"

"We are on a mission to find the sacred pink elephant that roams the jungle," replies the head Nobber.
"This is a dangerous place to be, there are native cannibals who will try to kill and eat you." I tell them to go back. They all start laughing.

"What's so funny?" I ask.
The head Nobber then explains. "We'll be OK, because the natives don't like it up em." In panic I reach for my trusty jungle knife as I back off into the safety of the dense undergrowth.

I climb a tree and watch as the Nobu monks continue with their journey and disappear into the jungle. After waiting up the tree for six hours (just to be on the safe side) I climb down and continue with my own journey towards the twin-peaked mountain.

I check my position, there should be a track leading towards the twin-peaked mountain to my right. I look closer and see broken twigs and grass in front of me. I roll out old yo-yo head against the dense undergrowth. The bushes part, and the trail then opens up in front of me, at the same time a giant razor sharp pendulum swings down slicing old yo-yo head in two.

THE GOLDEN GOBBLER 1

It is a booby trapped entrance to the hidden trail I have been searching for. I retrieve both bits of old yo-yo head and tape him back together. I check around for more hidden dangers, and then set off along the trail cautiously reeling out yo-yo head as I go.

I can hear the sounds of many voices ahead. I get off the trail and sneak closer. There is a clearing ahead with people moving around. I recognise the tribe from the ribbons in their hair and the wooden shoes on their feet. "Bollocks!" They are the Clitclop tribe who sacrifice their prisoners as an offering to their God, Clitoria at a ceremony called the Clitclop Hop. In the centre is a stone altar with someone already tied spread-eagled on it ready to be sacrificed.

The Clitclops are dancing in groups around the altar beating sticks together and ringing bells. They remind me of the ancient ones called Morris dancers who inhabit an island many miles away that was once called Great Britain, but it is now called the UK, which is short for " Fucked." This island is now inhabited by over forty thousand different tribes from many countries. The inhabitants were recently asked if they wanted to change the currency of the country to the Euro. They all declined, saying. "They were more than happy with the Giro."

I focus my binoculars, and take a closer look at the poor unfortunate to be sacrificed. To my amazement it is Goldie on the altar; she must have survived the fall over the cliff edge.

THE GOLDEN GOBBLER 1

Standing over her is the executioner with a large axe ready to chop her head off. The chief of the Clitclops raises a white handkerchief and the executioner raises his axe above Goldie's head. No time to lose now, I aim my rifle and fire an exploding round into the mouth of the executioner. His head explodes into a thousand pieces as the axe falls and cuts off his toes. "He will need a bandage for that." I laugh as I start machine gunning the rest of them. More sounds of gunfire are coming from the other side of the clearing. Some other attackers are also shooting at the Clitclops. "Who the hell can they be? I wonder. "

Soon all is quiet and I shout over to the other attackers. "Who are you?" I hear a voice reply.

"It is Jake the Snake here with some friends."

"Ok, go into the clearing and check if there is anyone still alive." I reply.

This bunch of bandits are bounty hunters, mercenaries, and killers. Jake the Snake is a slimy two-faced character. I had met him and some of the others at the Old Barnyard Saloon, a drinking and gambling joint that has a popular brothel above. This is situated in a lawless place called The Big River Settlement, many miles from here.

There is also among the gang Fred the Shred, a toad faced killer who throws people alive into his portable shredding machine that he takes with him on his journeys. He does this just for the fun of it. Then there is Benny bend-over, a revolting rat faced character who would kill his grandmother for a fiver.

THE GOLDEN GOBBLER 1

Among those I have met before is Marshmallow Dick, who is an unsuccessful bank robber, along with his mad drinking associate called Cardsharp Kev, who cheats at card games. He frequently gets caught out, and ends up getting a severe beating. And then there is Unsteady Teddy, who drinks four bottles of whisky a day. This has aided him in gun fights as he dodges the bullets while drunk and staggering about from side to side.

Finally among those I recognise, is Sid the Sneak, there is something of the night about this character. In the hours of darkness, he skulks around menacingly in alleyways. Usually someone ends up with their throat cut and minus their money. He has two fingers missing from one hand as a result of Six Gun Sarah shooting them off when he tried to steal a drink from behind the bar when she was serving.

There are five others who I don't recognise but you wouldn't introduce them to the local vicar. There are a few Clitclops wounded, but barely alive. Fred the Shred starts up his portable shredding machine. He starts sliding the wounded down the chute. The screams of the Clitclops fill the air. Jake the Snake cuts Goldie free from the altar, then he ties her hands together. I call out to him.

"What's on ere then Jake?"

"We will be paid a lot of reward money when we take her back to the Big River Settlement," was his reply. Goldie still has a gag around her mouth, but she is struggling and trying to tell me something. I am beginning to get an uneasy feeling about this situation.

THE GOLDEN GOBBLER 1

"Who wants her returned?" I ask.

"Why her loving relatives," replies Jake the Snake.

Goldie has pulled the gag off and cries out, "Don't believe him, they want to take me back to be a sex slave, help me!" she pleads.

Fred the Shred then shouts out, "Bring Casey Jones over here and I will feed him into my shredding machine." The others then point their guns in my direction. I have taken a severe dislike to toad faced Fred. I had already slid my trusty jungle knife from its sheath and it was now under Jake the Snakes chin. I shout out to the gang.

"Drop your weapons or your leader dies and there will be no money for you lot." "He's bluffing, shoot him," shouts rat faced Benny.

I fire a bullet into Benny bend-overs good eye; he lost the other one during a knife fight with Mad Mary from Macedonia when she caught him cheating at poker. "He's not bluffing, drop you guns." orders Jake the Snake. I can see a pool of piss form around his boots as he pleads for his life. The rest of the gang then lower their weapons and drop them on the ground.

Big mistake on their part, I drive my razor sharp jungle knife upwards through Jake the Snakes mouth, it enters his brain killing him instantly. At the same time my trusty machine-gun is in action, and I mow down the others. Unsteady Teddy is the only one left standing. I am amazed that the bullets have missed him and he is still wobbling from side to side shouting out "Drink, drink, more drink."

THE GOLDEN GOBBLER 1

Marshmallow Dick, Cardsharp Kev and Fred the Shred are also unharmed. They are lying on the ground covering their heads with their hands. I rush over and tie them up. I grab Fred by his hair and drag him over to his shredding machine. I tie him to the machine slide with his feet facing the shredding cutters.

"Now you can have a taste of your own medicine." Fred the Shred is screaming, pleading for mercy. I am just about to press the forward button on the slide, when Goldie cries out.

"Please don't Master."
I am touched by her compassion after the ordeals she has been through, but this is short lived as she finishes by saying,

"Let me feed Fred into the machine."

"OK, I will show you how to operate the buttons."
She squeals with delight, jumping up and down clapping her hands. I watch while my mad companion gleefully feeds Fred into the machine, slowly a little bit at a time to prolong the agony. Fred the Shreds scream now fills the air. Goldie's squeals of happiness also echo every time she feeds him in and out of the shredder. The others are begging for their lives. I still have not decided what to do with them yet. "Maybe Goldie can have them."

I leave her to play with the buttons as I go and look for the trail to the temple. I discover a track which leads me through the trees to another clear area. At the edge of the clearing I see a wonderful sight ahead of me. There is a crystal clear lake with the twin peaked mountain on the far side. The scenery is breath-taking.

THE GOLDEN GOBBLER 1

I hear a sound from behind. Goldie is stood there dripping with blood that had sprayed from Fred the Shred. "Me velly glateful you save me again Master," she says as she strips off.

"Wait, first get cleaned up and wash your cloot in yonder lake." She gets into the lake and I follow, but firstly, I inflate my large rubber duck I have affectionately named Fuk. I then tie my machine gun to it for our safety and protection when we are in the water.

While we are frolicking in the lake and my golden skinned companion is being "velly glateful." I see a ripple in the water ahead. Something is approaching. I throw Goldie up onto the bank when she is on the upward bounce. I can see the eyes on the surface now; it is a crocodile closing in fast. I only just make it out of the lake in time as the giant jaws open and clamp shut on Fuk the duck and my machine-gun.

The crocodile disappears in a death roll. Quick as a flash I yank the fishing line that I had earlier tied to the trigger of my machine gun. Loud noises follow, the water turns red as the crocodile floats to the surface with many holes in its head. I reel in my line; my machine gun is undamaged, but poor old Fuk the duck has had it, he has been bitten in two and will float no more. Still we can have crocodile stew for dinner! This is when I find out if Goldie can cook, if not she has to go.

THE GOLDEN GOBBLER 1

We go back to the Clitclop camp-site, taking part of the crocodile to cook for dinner. I see one of the prisoners is missing. I then ask Goldie.

"Where is Marshmallow Dick, has he escaped?"

"No, he kept on making belching noises and called me an old cow, so I slid him into the shredding machine after Fred the Shred. The machine is not working now, if you can fix it, then I can put Unsteady Teddy and Cardsharp Kev into it." She laughs hysterically as she looks over at the now terrified Cardsharp Kev who is calling out in fear. He pleads for his life.

"No, no, no, have a turn of the cards to decide our fate." cries Cardsharp Kev. I like a bit of a gamble so I am interested in his plea. "What do you propose?"

Cardsharp Kev then outlines the bet. "Deal two hands of cards, if you have the highest hand then we will accept whatever fate that you decide, but please not the shredding machine. On the other hand, if we have the highest hand, then you set us free and we will take the girl back for the reward money. I will put half into an account for you to collect later. Unsteady Teddy is nodding in agreement. "I will think about it, but first we eat, the crocodile is nearly cooked and I am hungry.

As we wait my mind drifts back to the Old Barnyard Saloon where I first had the misfortune to clap eyes on this bunch of bandits. Six Gun Sarah is the proprietor, she is a wild fearsome woman who fires her colt 45 in the air to close the premises; at the same time she places a shotgun on the bar. If after two minutes any customers have not left the establishment, she then opens fire and blasts them with the shotgun .

THE GOLDEN GOBBLER 1

She also has an evil sense of humour, in that sometimes she pretends to fire her colt 45 and blasts away with the shotgun anyway. Bendy Wendy works in the brothel above. She is very popular with the customers; this is due to her ability to touch her ears with her toes. Northern Nell is another favourite with the clients. Her speciality is discipline, dishing out pain and punishment with her assortment of whips, chains and a baseball bat. She relishes in this role, but gets carried away sometimes. Recently she beat two of the punters to death with her baseball bat.

Six Gun Sarah was furious at the loss of custom, and decreed that the baseball bat must be covered with leather to prevent any serious injury in the future.

Now back to the decision on the fate of Cardsharp Kev and Unsteady Teddy. I tell them I accept their plea. I shuffle the cards and deal out three cards for them and three cards for me.

"The highest hand wins, now turn your cards." Cardsharp Kev turns a pair of Jacks and a ten of Clubs. I turn a pair of Aces and a three of Spades.

"Sorry gentlemen you lose. The good news is you won't be going into the shredder, the bad news is you will be hanged from yonder tree." Unsteady Teddy is pleading for mercy. "Whit have ah done then, ah've no done anything wrang." He looks at Goldie for support. She laughs and wraps a cord round his neck trying to throttle him. I quickly run over and stop her. "We will do this properly, go and fetch the horse and cart that Fred the Shred carried his shredding machine in, we will use it for the hanging."

THE GOLDEN GOBBLER 1

I toss a coin to see who goes first. Cardsharp Kev is the unlucky one. I put him into the cart beside the tree. The hanging rope is in place around a branch. I place the noose around his neck and tighten the knot.

"Any last request?" I ask.

"No, no, no," he answers in terror.

I signal to Goldie to drive the cart forward. Cardsharp Kev drops off the end of the cart, a loud snap follows as his neck breaks and he dies instantly. "A clean kill," I am happy with that.

"Now for Unsteady Teddy." He is still struggling and wobbling from side to side. I get the rope around his neck and throw him into the cart. I then secure the rope to the tree. I tighten the noose.

"Any last request Teddy" I ask him.

"Yes, I wid jist like tae say ....

Before he could finish, Goldie drives the cart forward and Unsteady Teddy drops off the end. What followed was truly amazing, there was no snap of the neck, he bounced up and down by his neck like a bungee jumper. "His neck must be made of rubber I thought."

When he stopped bouncing, I could see he was still breathing. He has cheated death again. He could not be shot and he could not be hanged. I decide to finish him off for good. I give him the full blast from my flame thrower. As soon as the flame makes contact, and with the alcohol fumes he is breathing, Unsteady Teddy turns into a huge fireball with bits of burning flesh sparking in all directions. Goldie is jumping up and down clapping her hands and screeching with delight.

"I love fireworks" she cries out.

THE GOLDEN GOBBLER 1

Soon it is over and all that is left of Unsteady Teddy is a small pile of ash on the ground. Goldie goes over and kneels down in front of his remains as if in prayer. She has a heart after all. My belief is short lived, for suddenly she lowers her head and blows Teddy's ashes along the ground, then she utters. "That's the blow job you were always asking me for," followed by hysterical laughter.

My golden skinned companion is looking very sexy and appealing. I decide to give her one. I call out to her. "Goldie, do you fancy a shag or what?" "Yes" she replies and runs over to me. I take her in my arms and kiss her stiffly. I carry her over to a fallen tree by the lakes edge. I think to myself, "This setting is very romantic," as I bend her over the tree and back-scuttle her till she squeaks.

I leave Goldie stretched across the fallen tree, I have to get across the lake to the twin peaked-mountain, so I get to work building a raft. I soon have the raft finished. I have made it from bamboo, and tied together with roots from the undergrowth. Out of the corner of my eye I see something gliding along on top of the lake. I quickly take aim with my rifle, pointing at the approaching object.

It is a canoe and I recognise the occupant. I breathe a sigh of relief, for it is my old friend Randy Dandy; a beaver trapping soldier of fortune. I call out to him. "Welcome Randy what brings you to these parts, I suppose you are beaver hunting?" He replies "Yes, among other things," as he casts his eyes on Goldie, who is still bent over the fallen tree.

THE GOLDEN GOBBLER 1

He gets out of the canoe and we shake hands. Then quick as a flash he is over and plugged into Goldie. I laugh and shake my head. "You don't miss an opportunity Randy Dandy you rascal."

They both appear to be enjoying the occasion and oblivious to all around them, so I decide this is the time to leave, and get rid of my companion at the same time, as the crocodile she cooked was crap.

I finish loading up the raft and silently set sail across the lake. On reaching the other side I hide the raft and set off towards the twin peaked mountain to find the secret temple that holds the Golden Gobbler within.

THE GOLDEN GOBBLER 1

CHAPTER 3

ANIMAL MAGIC

I have covered about five miles when I hear hysterical piercing laughter ahead. I approach with caution. Through the dense green undergrowth I see three figures that appear to be half human and half animal; it looks like generations of inbreeding have produced such creatures.

Lying on her back laughing hysterically is a hobbit like female with legs pointed up in the air. Astride her is a male creature with a head like a wild boar, he is poking away furiously. Lying beside them is another bearded male of crab like form and appearance, no doubt waiting for his turn. The female is indulging in what I can only think is some kind of primitive sexual foreplay, for between hysterical laughter, she is picking her nose and wiping her finger over the bearded creatures body.

I can watch this horrendous bestial activity no longer, I remember an old sea dog who went by the name of "Don't go there Joe" and his favourite saying, "You put your prick where I wouldn't put my walking stick." This sight would offend the walking stick. I make my way around the rutting trio, and continue on my way. I press on hoping to encounter no further dangers.

THE GOLDEN GOBBLER 1

Back at the Old Barnyard Saloon, the proprietor, Six Gun Sarah has just finished cleaning her colt 45 and is loading the bullets preparing for the arrival of the night time customers.

Suddenly the swing doors are flung open and two customers stagger in. It is Dick Heady, the mad country cousin of Unsteady Teddy, and with him is Coconut Kev, the twin brother of Cardsharp Kev.

Dick Heady shouts out. "We can't find any sign of Unsteady Teddy or Cardsharp Kev, or any of the others. They have disappeared without trace." He is angry and fires his gun into the ceiling.

Pom- Pom the bartender tries to turn and disappear from the bar. The steely grip of Six Gun Sarah's hand around his neck freezes him to the spot. "Stay here and stand your ground," orders Sarah to the terrified bartender.
Pom-Pom is shaking like a wobbling jelly on a plate , he has one hand behind his back protecting his rear. A bead of sweat runs from his forehead into his eye, causing him to wink in the direction of Dick Heady.

When Dick catches sight of him winking, he starts to mellow. A smile and a shining glint sparkle from his teeth as he casts his eyes over Pom-Pom.

Coconut Kev then starts to mutter something when Six Gun Sarah silences him. "Shut up fool," she utters. Coconut Kev looks down at his boots.

31

THE GOLDEN GOBBLER 1

A loud cracking noise, followed by a blood curdling scream is heard coming from the mouth of Dick Heady. Northern Nell had sliced off Dick's ear with one of her whips. At the same time a gong like clang is heard as Scullery Sam's cast iron frying pan connects with Coconut Kev sending him unconscious to the floor.

The muzzle of Six Gun Sarah's colt 45 is pressed firmly against his other ear. "Get out of here Dick Heady or you'll soon be deady; and take the fool with you" orders Sarah.

The sweat is now running down Dick Heady's brow into his eye causing him to wink also. By this time both Pom-Pom the bartender and Dick Heady are winking like a flashing beacon. Then there is a dull thud followed by another high pitched scream as Dick falls to the floor.

Two Gun Tex had driven his boot firmly between Dick's legs and connected with his bollocks. He had done this deed as he was not impressed that his poker game had been interrupted.

Tex picks up Dick Heady's severed ear and puts in in Dick's pink waistcoat pocket. The other customers then help Tex throw the two troublemakers out of the saloon.

"Is everyone OK" asks Six Gun Sarah. "Yes, I just have to wash the blood and coconut fibres off the frying pan and I'll cook something to eat" replies Scullery Sam.

Northern Nell is smiling and happily licking the blood off the end of her whip.

THE GOLDEN GOBBLER 1

Bendy Wendy had been entertaining Merlin the Scalp hunter in the brothel above and had come down to see what the commotion was about. She is holding her knickers in one hand, and a pair of scissors in the other.

Six Gun Sarah tells her it is all over and to go back upstairs to her client. Merlin also calls for her to get back upstairs.

"I'm coming" shouts Bendy Wendy. "So will I be when you get back up here" was the reply from Merlin the Scalp hunter.

Tricky Tracey the bookkeeper had been upstairs with Lulu the Scribe. He appears with a shotgun looking important.

"Typical Tricky Tracy, you appear when all the action has finished, get back upstairs to Lulu, you tosser" screams Six Gun Sarah. Tricky scuttles back upstairs in haste.

All is quiet in the bar as Bendy Wendy re-appears . She walks bow legged towards the bar looking like John Wayne after a long day on horseback.

"Merlin the Scalp Hunter wants to pay his brothel fee with an old smelly scalp he had cut off someone's head," she complains.

Merlin had followed behind her and throws the blooded scalp onto the bar. "This scalp is worth twenty dollars, so ten dollars fee for shagging Bendy Wendy, and ten dollars for three fingers of red eye. (slang for brandy) That will make us quits," says the brave scalp hunter.

THE GOLDEN GOBBLER 1

A twitch starts in Six Gun Sarah's eye; which is a bad sign.

Quick as lightening, she shoves the barrel of her Colt 45 deep into Merlin's mouth. At the same time she rips off the gold chain he is wearing around his neck.

Sarah is furious but still calmly says to Merlin, "The gold chain is worth eighty dollars, so that will be a twenty dollars fee for shagging Bendy Wendy, ten dollars charge for three fingers of red eye, and fifty dollars to me for not blowing your head off. Do you agree to my terms?
Merlin the Scalp Hunter is quaking in his boots, he nods furiously in agreement as his teeth chatter against the barrel of Sarah's gun.

Six Gun Sarah pours Merlin his three shots of brandy." Drink this, stick that scalp where the sun don't shine and get out of here."

Merlin Quickly finishes his drink and starts to leave the premises when he lets out a withering squeal. Bendy Wendy had thrown his scalping scissors after him and one of the blades had stuck in the back of his neck.

"Bastards," he screams, as blood pours from his wound. He reaches for his gun, but Mac the Chef is on his case, he swings his chopper at Merlin the Scalp Hunter's head.

The chopper strikes Merlin just above his eyes. The force of the blow from the penis causes a deep red weal across Merlin's forehead. He drops to the floor stunned.

THE GOLDEN GOBBLER 1

Mac the Chef quickly disarms Merlin and bundles him out of the door.

Bendy Wendy is still waddling about when Sarah stops her. "You can't walk around like that, go and have a lie down till your legs straighten out. Pom-Pom, you help Wendy upstairs"

When Pom-Pom had not returned after about twenty minutes, Sarah decides to go up and see what is delaying him. When she enters Bendy Wendy's room she sees Pom-Pom holding Wendy's legs wheelbarrow fashion, his trousers at his feet. He is standing between her legs, poking away like a coal engine stoker.

Six Gun Sarah is furious and screams out. "No Freebies, I've told you before Pom-Pom. Get back down to the bar." Pom-Pom protests his innocence. "I'm only helping to straighten out her legs." A gurgling noise follows as Northern Nell's whip wraps around his neck, a squelching sound is heard as she then yanks him clear of Bendy Wendy.

Six Gun Sarah ventures outdoors to cool down and get some fresh air. While she is sitting in her rocking chair she sees the silhouette of a horse and rider approaching slowly. As they get closer, she notices the rider is naked from the waist down. She looks up and recognises the face, it is Buff-arse Bill the bear hunter.

" How are you Bill, going in for a drink?" Yes thanks Sarah, but first I'm going up to the brothel, I have been away on my own for six months now and I need a shag. Who is available tonight?"

THE GOLDEN GOBBLER 1

Well you can't have Bendy Wendy, as her legs haven't straightened out yet. You can have Northern Nell or Winnie the Glutton," answered Sarah.

"The last time I had Northern Nell, she took the skin off my back and nearly broke my neck. I suppose then, I'll have Winnie the Glutton this time." Bill ponders for a moment. "On second thoughts, I'll take the pain and have Northern Nell."

Buff-arse Bill swings down from his saddle, his longhorn flapping in the wind. Six Gun Sarah is impressed and says to Bill. "Never mind the brothel, come with me." With that she takes hold of Bill by his longhorn and leads him into the empty Longhorn bar at the side of the saloon. Bill didn't need any coaxing, he soon has Six Gun Sarah stripped naked and bent over a table.

Tricky Tracy had just left the saloon when he hears the sound of moans and squeals coming from the Longhorn bar.

He opens the door and sees Buff-arse Bill merrily thrusting away and Six Gun Sarah biting the end of the table.

"Can I join in" asks Tricky. "Sod off you tosser" replies Sarah and fires a warning shot at him. The bullet whizzes past and parts Tricky Tracy's hair. He lets out a girlie scream and runs away into the darkness of the night.

THE GOLDEN GOBBLER 1

CHAPTER 4

THE LAST LEG

On reaching the twin peaked mountain, Casey Jones begins the search for the entrance to the secret temple. He can find no openings or any sign of hidden doors. After three days searching, Casey gets frustrated and throws old yo-yo head against the mountain wall. And when old yo-yo head makes contact, right before his very eyes he watches as the entrance suddenly appears, old yo-yo head has triggered the mechanism to the hidden door.

He look inside, there are steps leading up to a round stone platform. This is the secret temple for sure. There are many shapes and figures drawn on the walls, depicting ancient warriors and events of years gone by. Casey scans the area, no sign of the Golden Gobbler. "She must be here somewhere."

He climbs the stairway up to the stone platform. When he reaches the top, he sees the stone has strange writing around the edge and what appear to be stars. Then as Casey is standing in the centre of the stone platform, he becomes engulfed in a blue light. He tries to move, but it is impossible, he cannot move however hard he tries. "Is this the end, where will fate and destiny lead to now?" asks Casey.

THE GOLDEN GOBBLER 1

Casey relates what happens next.
The blue light disappears; I can feel a gentle breeze against my face. There is a white mist in front of me that is beginning to clear. I look upwards; there is a clear blue sky with what appears to be two suns in the distance.

There are also six large planets, one which has a ring of many colours surrounding it. Wherever, and whatever this place is, it is not planet earth. The mist has cleared. In front of me I see the statue of the Golden Gobbler. She stands about seven feet tall, with diamonds and gold gleaming in the bright light of this place.

At the foot of the statue standing around waiting to meet me, are some of the explorers who had gone on the same quest as myself and never returned. I recognise many of them from their newspaper photographs, some dating back over two hundred years. But the most surprising thing of all is that none of them appear to have aged since they disappeared.

"My quest has ended, I have indeed found
the Golden Gobbler, but at what cost?"

THE END

To

Happy Birthday

Printed in Great Britain
by Amazon